For Casper

Wishing you a magical life

Tim Forest

Does Not Have

Stanley Stickle ~~Has~~ A Girlfriend

By

Trevor Forest

Dog Eared Books 2012

Special thanks to Maureen Vincent-Northam for providing her excellent editing skills. Thanks also to Marie Fullerton for the fabulous cover and illustrations.
I would also like to give a big, virtual stroke to my Springer Spaniels, Molly and Maisie, who were such good girls while I was writing this book.

Trevor Forest 2012

Stanley Stickle HATES Mondays

'You were so lucky being off sick, Stanley, you missed the Big Test.'

Stanley smiled to himself. It hadn't been easy but he had managed to get ill and take a fortnight off school. He turned to his best friend. 'Was it really bad?'

'Dreadful,' said George, 'the worst test ever.'

Stanley craned his neck to look over George's shoulder. Then he turned and looked up the street the other way. 'Hurry up bus,' he muttered.

'Looking for someone?' asked George with a sly grin.

Stanley shuffled his feet and looked at the floor. 'Me? No, I'm just watching for the bus, that's all.'

'You seem very eager to get to school,' said George. 'Are you sure you're not still poorly. Or are you just keen to see someone?'

Stanley wanted to say he was hoping *NOT* to see someone; that someone being Soppy Sonia. Instead, he just shook his head. 'Ah, here it comes now.'

When the bus pulled up at the stop, the orderly queue suddenly exploded as everyone leapt forward to try to get to their favourite seat. George and Stanley usually sat near the back.

George managed to get on first. He hurtled down the aisle and threw himself into the window seat four rows from the back. Stanley got stuck behind Limping Liam who had to come to school with his foot in a plaster cast after breaking it when he accidentally kicked a goal post in football training. Stanley couldn't work out how anyone could accidentally kick a goal post. It's not like you don't know it's there; it's eight feet high and painted white.

Stanley shuffled down the bus behind Limping Liam wondering why everyone was grinning at him. When he was half way down the aisle, he found out as a soft voice called to him.

'Sit here with me, Stanley.'

Stanley groaned. *Soppy Sonia must have got on the bus at an earlier stop.*

'I've saved you a seat, Stanley.' Sonia removed her bag from the seat next to her and patted it.

Stanley's mind raced like a formula one car on a test track. He would rather eat a massive plate of soggy cabbage than sit with Soppy Sonia on the school bus.

'Err, sorry, Sonia,' he gabbled. 'I've got something to sort out with George.' Stanley almost knocked Limping Liam into Sonia's arms as he pushed past and hurled himself into his regular seat. He hoped George hadn't seen the incident.

George had. 'What did Soppy Sonia want?'

'Um, she er, wants to know if I collect stamps,' replied Stanley. 'She's brought her album to school or something. I'm not sure why she thought I'd be interested.'

George looked surprised. 'Oh, I thought she was asking you to sit with her.'

Stanley forced a laugh. 'Me, sit with Soppy Sonia, why would I want to do that?'

George smiled and looked out of the window.

At school, Stanley was first off the bus. He raced for the boys toilets and locked himself in a cubicle. Five minutes later there was a knock on the door; it was George.

'Stanley?'

'Yes?'

'Why are you hiding?'

'I'm not actually *hiding*, I er, I just don't want someone to see me.'

'That's the same thing isn't it?'

'Similar,' agreed Stanley.

'Soppy Sonia's telling everyone you're her new boyfriend,' whispered George.

'*She's what!*'

'SOPPY SONIA IS TELLING…'

'Okay, I heard,' hissed Stanley. 'No need to tell the world.'

'I think the world knows about it already,' said George. 'She's got a crowd of people around her in the playground. She was whispering to her friends about it while you were off sick but no one believed her then.'

Stanley clicked the bolt back and came slowly out of the cubicle.

'I'm finished,' he said. 'My life is over.'

'What's been going on?' asked George. 'Why is she saying that?'

Stanley's shoulders slumped. 'It's a long story. She just got hold of the wrong end of the stick, that's all. I'll try to sort it out.'

'You'd better hurry,' said George. 'Some of the girls are planning a wedding.'

Stanley walked into the playground like a condemned man heading for the gallows. He spotted the crowd around Sonia as soon as he left the toilet block. He couldn't miss it, half the school was there.

When Stanley was spotted, a complete silence came over the playground. Stanley looked at the scores of faces staring at him. Caitlin and Rebecca held their hands to their mouths to stop themselves giggling. The silence held as Stanley made his lonely way across the asphalt. It was broken when Kieran Kyte started singing.

'Here comes the bride, fifty inches wide. Here comes the groom, stinking of perfume.'

Within seconds, every child in the playground joined in. Stanley glared at the grinning Sonia and decided he'd been humiliated enough. He changed his mind about talking to her and headed for the classroom.

At registration, Mrs Oscar the drama teacher came into the class to ask for volunteers.

'We're really short of boys for the school production of Oliver. Would anyone like to volunteer?'

Molly and Maisie Springer, the twins, pushed their hands into the air in unison. 'Me, me,' they echoed.

'We have enough girls for now, thank you,' said Mrs Oscar. 'It's the boys we're short of.' Her eyes scanned the room hoping to see an arm in the air. The boys looked at everything except the teacher. Stanley found a very interesting ink blob on his desk and studied it intently. He would rather walk barefoot over a field of stinging nettles than be in the school play.

Mrs Oscar sighed. 'I suppose this means that girls will have to play the boys' parts again this year.'

'ME! ME!' The twins pushed their hands into the air again.

Mrs Oscar sighed again and jotted down their names. Molly and Maisie did, and said, everything together; it was like having a living echo in the class.

Mr Strap, the form teacher, began to work his way through the register. He called out names and the children responded with, 'here Sir.' When he got to Stanley the class giggled. When he got to Sonia, the class erupted.

'What's so funny?' he asked.

'She's going to be Sonia Stickle soon,' said Caitlin. 'They're getting married.'

The class howled with laughter again.

Stanley risked a sideways look at Sonia. She was beaming. Her smile went from ear to ear.

Mr Strap looked puzzled and continued the roll call. Stanley studied the ink blob again and desperately tried to think up a plan.

Stanley Stickle HAS a girlfriend

Stanley's day got worse when he found out that he had to take the Big Test after all. Mr Strap called him out to the front of the class after registration.

'Stanley you are to go to the hall and wait for Mrs Crotchet. She will supervise you while you do the test. You can resume your normal lessons when you finish.'

Stanley was appalled.

'But, but, I haven't had the extra homework to help prepare for it like everyone else.'

Mr Strap was unsympathetic. 'Would you like some extra homework, Stanley, I can arrange it?'

Stanley thought about it for ten millionths of a second and shook his head. He hated homework even more than he hated big tests. He would rather stick his hand in a wasp's nest than ask for extra homework.

Mrs Crotchet, the music teacher, was waiting for him when he entered the hall. She had set up a desk and chair at the front of the room facing the stage.

'Hello, Stanley, aren't you a lucky boy? You almost missed out on this.'

Stanley mumbled something about winning the lottery and slumped down in the chair. Mrs Crochet placed a wad of paper held together with a staple, upside down on the desk. 'Don't look so dejected, Stanley, there are only six sheets and you've got ninety minutes to do it.'

Stanley thought the pile of papers looked about the same size as a phone book.

At nine thirty, Mrs Crochet pressed a button on the clock on her desk and told Stanley he could turn over the test paper. 'You are not allowed to leave the room or talk to anyone while you are sitting the exam,' she warned.

Stanley looked around the empty hall. *Talk to who?* He turned over the paper and wrote his name on the top of the top sheet. His eyes skimmed the first question. It was all about a girl called Cherry who had fifteen apples and gave some to a friend called Clementine.

He stuck his chin in his hands. *Is this a maths test or a cookery class?* Stanley worked through the questions quickly. He was quite clever in a lazy sort of way. After an hour, he had almost finished but he didn't want to go back to his usual lesson to face the class until he had worked out a plan to deal with Soppy Sonia.

It had all seemed such a brilliant idea at the time. Stanley had agreed to give Soppy Sonia a thirty-second kiss and be her boyfriend in the hope of catching chickenpox from her so he could miss the Big Test. It had all backfired. He didn't even catch chickenpox. His horrible sister, Stacey, had given him scarlet fever instead, which was much worse.

Stanley's eyes suddenly lit up. That was it; scarlet fever! He already had a plan. A wonderful plan, a plan so magnificent it would go down in history as the plan that made all other plans look puny. If only he could remember what it was? Stanley thought up the plan between bouts of being sick and taking medicine to bring his temperature down. He had written it down on a bit of tissue paper and hidden it somewhere in his room. Stanley racked his brains but couldn't remember where. He'd had lots of strange dreams while he was ill and he couldn't remember any of them properly.

Stanley finished the test, handed the paper to Mrs Crochet and walked back to his class with a smile on his face. Hidden in his room was the mega plan that would rid him of Soppy Sonia for ever. All he had to do now was find it.

*****

When Stanley walked across the playground to get the bus at three thirty, he found two lines of pupils forming a guard of honour near the school gates. As he walked by there were catcalls and whistles.

'Hurry up, Stanley, she's waiting.'

'Here comes the bride, ninety inches wide.'

'Here comes the groom, stinking of perfume.'

Caitlin and Rebecca giggled as Stanley skulked past.

'We're going to be bridesmaids, Stanley,' said Caitlin.

Rebecca giggled again. 'You have to wear a pink suit.'

Stanley went bright red and stared at the floor.

Molly and Maisie, the twins, were waiting just outside the gates.

'Tell Sonia to throw the bouquet to me, Stanley,' said Molly.

'No, throw the bouquet to me,' said Maisie.

Stanley stopped.

'Do you two always have to repeat each other?'

'We don't,' said Molly and Maisie, together.

Stanley shook his head and walked on. Sonia was waiting for him on the street, wearing a grin the size of a dinner plate. She held out her bag to Stanley.

Stanley was horrified. He would rather be seen wearing a Rovers football strip than be seen carrying Sloppy Sonia's bag. He ignored her outstretched arm and started to walk towards the bus stop.

'I could tell them just how long our big kiss was, Stanley,' she hissed.

Stanley thought about it. Things were bad enough already but if they knew the whole truth it could get a lot worse. He reached out and took the bag from Sonia and threw it grumpily over his shoulder. As Sonia took his arm, fifty mobile phone cameras snapped pictures.

*****

Stanley suffered a horrendous bus ride and was jeered and booed when he got off the bus at Sonia's stop. As they walked, Sonia twittered on about what they could do together at the weekend. Stanley didn't hear a word of it. He was working on a speech that he would deliver at Sonia's gate. He had rehearsed it in his mind twenty times on the bus. It began with, *Sorry Sonia, it's been fun, but it's over.*

As he neared Sonia's house Stanley could hear Angus and Michael Dunbar sniggering behind him. At the gate, Sonia leaned forward and pursed her lips in front of Stanley's face. Stanley's eyes almost popped out of his head. *She wasn't expecting another kiss, was she?* He would rather wrestle a grizzly bear with toothache than kiss Soppy Sonia again, especially with Angus and Michael watching.

Stanley forgot all about his speech and took the only option he had left. He dropped Sonia's bag and ran for it. He didn't stop running until he reached his own gate. He arrived at the front door, hot, bothered but determined. This had to stop, and it had to stop tomorrow. Somewhere in his room was the answer to his prayers. The biggest and best plan he had ever had. Stanley raced upstairs to his room and began the search.

Stanley gets more bad news

Stanley searched the obvious places first. He looked in his bedside drawer and under the bed. Then he bounced up and down on his bed while he checked the top of the wardrobe. He flipped through every book on his bookcase in case he had hidden it inside one of them but he found nothing except for an old Rangers match ticket stub that he used as a bookmark. Finally, he looked in his top-secret place.

Stanley checked the landing and stairs to make sure his sister wasn't hanging around, and closed his bedroom door. He pulled the curtains shut, grabbed his torch and tiptoed across the floor to the human skeleton model that hung from the ceiling on a thin piece of rope. Stanley carefully unhinged the top of the skull and fished out the contents. There was the photo of his sister with a mud pack on her face that he promised he'd destroyed but was saving up for emergency blackmail, his rare football card swaps for the set everyone was collecting, his champion 'sixer' conker, from last autumn and a broken watch, that he hadn't told his mother about yet.

Stanley placed his treasures back in the skull, clipped back the top and opened the curtains again. He sat on the bed and scratched his head. *What had he done with it?* He could vaguely remember writing something and he could definitely remember that it was the best plan he had ever devised, but he couldn't remember where he had put it.

After another twenty minutes of serious thought, Stanley had a brainwave and lifted up the mattress. There, in the middle of the base, was the answer to all his problems. The best plan any boy had ever thought up, ever. Stanley picked it up carefully, dropped the mattress back into place, checked the door again and sat on the edge of the bed. He unfolded the piece of paper with shaking hands, closed his eyes, issued a quick prayer, and stared at the scribbled note.

Tie Soppy Sonia to the back of a giant armadillo, stick on a first-class stamp and post it to Pantsland.

Stanley shook his head and read it again. There was no mistake. He had actually written; *Tie Soppy Sonia to the back of a giant armadillo, stick on a first-class stamp and post it to Pantsland.*

Stanley groaned. He must really have been out of it when he wrote that. *There wasn't even a country called Pantsland, was there?* Stanley checked his atlas just in case, but his worst fears were confirmed.

Stanley put his head in his hands and groaned again. All his hopes had been tied up in that piece of paper. Stanley screwed it into a ball, threw it at the waste bin and went down for dinner. He needed another plan now and it had to be better than the best plan he'd ever planned in his life.

Stanley didn't think the day could possibly get any worse, but over dinner, Mum had more bad news for him.

'Stanley, I'd like you to pick up Gran's birthday flowers from the florist after school tomorrow.'

Stanley choked on his pasta. 'Flowers? … *FLOWERS!*'

Stacey, his sister, pointed a long finger at him, nodded her head, and grinned, smugly.

'I can't, Mum, I'm busy…'

'Tomorrow,' repeated Mum, 'after school.'

'But…'

'He doesn't want to miss the chance to walk his girlfriend home, that's what it is,' said the evil Stacey.'

Stanley choked again. The news was spreading.

'No excuses, Stanley,' said Mum. I don't have time to pick them up tomorrow and Stacey has hockey practice. They charge a fortune to deliver, so I'm sorry, but you're it.'

Stanley pushed his plate away, stuck his elbows on the table and placed his head in his hands.

Dad ruffled his hair and reached for teapot. 'Unlucky, Stanley.'

Stanley got up from the table and went back to his room.

*****

Stanley decided to walk to school the next day. He didn't want to risk the embarrassment of Soppy Sonia asking him to sit with her again and anyway, he needed to think. At breakfast, he had the germ of an idea and by the time he got to school, he had the basis of a new plan.

Plan A

Stanley went straight to the toilets and locked himself into a cubicle. Ten minutes later he walked through the taunts and catcalls with his head held high. His plan still needed some thought, but there was a good chance it would work.

Stanley found Sydney the Swot sitting on the grass checking his homework. He looked up as Stanley approached.

'Hello, Sydney, how are you?'

Sydney looked at Stanley suspiciously. It wasn't like Stanley to be polite unless he wanted something. 'Hello, Stanley, I'm good, thank you.'

Stanley sat down and made out he was interested in Sydney's homework. 'Hmm, maths, interesting.'

Sydney's suspicions went up a notch. He knew Stanley hated maths.'

Stanley smiled his best smile. 'You've always been good at maths, Sydney. I used to tell everyone that if they ever needed help with maths, you were just the person to see.'

Stanley pulled up a blade of grass and stuck it in the corner of his mouth. 'By the way, I meant to ask. Do you have a girlfriend, Sydney?'

'No, I wish I did. You're really lucky Stanley.'

'Lucky! I'm…' Stanley bit his lip just in time. 'Yes, I am lucky, very lucky. It's just that...well, I need someone I can trust.'

Sydney suddenly looked interested.

'I'm going to be really busy for a few nights and I need someone to stand in for me.'

Sydney looked puzzled. 'Stand in?'

'A substitute… sort of,' said Stanley.

'A substitute?'

'Yeah, could you be my sub with Sonia for a week or so while I'm busy, Sydney? I need someone I can trust and I know I can trust you. I wouldn't dream of asking anyone else.'

Sydney looked pleased. 'Oh you can trust me, Stanley. What would I have to do? I've never had a girlfriend before.'

Stanley looked away, grinned a sly grin, then turned back to Sydney with a serious look on his face.

'You would just need to walk her home, carry her bag and listen to her going on about ponies, that sort of thing.'

'That sounds easy enough. Does Sonia know about it?' asked Sydney.

'Er no, not yet. I didn't want to say anything to her until I knew I'd got a good sub,' said Stanley. 'I'll tell her soon; I'm going to be busy after school tonight so I need you to stand in for me.'

Stanley got to his feet as the bell rang. He smiled to himself as he walked past a group of pointing, giggling school friends and went into class for registration.

Later that morning Stanley received an unexpected bonus for his plan.

Stanley sat in class dreaming about scoring the winning goal for Deadenbury Rangers while the English teacher, Miss Lang, warbled on about past participles and irregular verbs. He was dragged out of his goal-scoring heroics by a whispered conversation to his left. Stanley looked down the line of desks just in time to see Soppy Sonia pass something to her best friend, Holly. Holly passed it to Caitlin who passed it to Rebecca. Rebecca nudged Kieran and nodded towards George. Kieran passed the note to George who passed it under the double-desk to Stanley.

Stanley unfolded the note and glanced down at it.

Meet me by the gates after school. S. XXX

Stanley choked. She put *KISSES* on the note. He would rather drink a bucket full of the worst tasting cough medicine on the planet than kiss Soppy Sonia again.

He was about to put the note in his pocket when he had an idea. Stanley refolded the paper and wrote, *Sydney*, on the outside. He nudged Allergy Alan and passed him the note. Alan passed it to Zitty Zac who passed it to Tall Tim, who passed it over his shoulder to Sydney.

When Stanley looked back, he saw Sydney beaming from ear to ear. Sydney tore a piece of paper from his jotter, wrote a quick note, folded it up, tapped Tall Tim on the shoulder and handed it to him. Tim passed it to Zac who passed it to Allergy Alan who passed it on to Stanley. Stanley had a quick look at the note under his desk.

I'll be there, look forward to seeing you. S. XXX

Stanley refolded the paper, winked at George and handed him the note. George gave it to Kieran who passed it to Rebecca. Rebecca gave it to Caitlin who passed it to Holly. Holly had a sneaky peek and handed it over to Soppy Sonia. Stanley took a quick peep along the line. Sonia spotted him, waved and blew him a kiss.

Stanley rubbed his hands together and smiled to himself. At the front of the class, Mrs Lang waffled on about something called a subjunctive. Stanley stared at the map of Tolkien's Middle Earth on the wall behind Mrs Lang's head and dreamed up an imaginary sword fight with a pair of Goblin warriors.

Stanley managed to avoid Soppy Sonia for the rest of the day by locking himself in the boys' toilets at break time. He ate his lunch in the caretaker's boiler house while Mr Handy was cleaning the windows in the art room. At three thirty Stanley raced to be first out of the school gates. He hid himself behind a large laurel in the shrubbery and waited for Sydney to show up.

He didn't have to wait long. Two minutes later Sydney hared through the playground stuffing books into his bag as he ran. He positioned himself by the school gate and checked his watch. Every thirty seconds or so he popped his head round the gate pillar to see if Sonia was coming. When he spotted her, he smoothed down his hair, scooped up a handful of daisies from the grass verge and hid them behind his back. Stanley switched on his mobile phone and lined up the shot.

When Soppy Sonia got to the gate, Sydney leapt forward and presented her with a limp bunch of daisies and bits of grass. Sonia smiled sweetly and took the flowers from Sydney. Across the road, in the laurels, Stanley took his picture and whispered *gotcha.*

Stanley waited until Sonia's back was turned and crept out of the shrubbery. He tiptoed across the road and stood behind Sydney and Sonia.

'But Stanley doesn't need a substitute, Sydney, you silly boy,' Sonia explained.

'Well, he asked me to stand in for him when he was busy,' said Sydney.

'Is he busy tonight?' asked Sonia.

'I don't know,' replied Sydney. 'I came because I got your note.'

'But I didn't send you a note, silly,' said Sonia.

Sydney pulled the crumpled paper from his pocket and handed it to Sonia. Sonia smoothed it out, read it and giggled into her hand.

'Oh, this wasn't meant for you, Sydney. I think there's been a mistake.'

She was silent for a moment so Stanley grabbed his chance and pushed his phone in front of her face.

‘Do you call this a mistake too?’

‘Oh, hello, Stanley, I wondered where you were.’

‘Never mind where I was,’ said Stanley. ‘How do you explain this?’ He pointed to the picture on the phone. ‘Meeting other boys at the school gates? That’s not on is it? I’m really upset about this, Sonia.’

‘Oh, Stanley, you’re jealous, that’s so sweet.’ Sonia leaned forward and kissed him on the cheek. ‘Wait till I tell Holly and the girls, they’ll be so thrilled.’

Stanley held the phone in the air. ‘But, but… flowers…’

‘Thank you for being such a sweetie, Stanley, I’ll see you in the morning. Must rush I’ve got an after-school embroidery class tonight.’

Sonia blew Stanley a kiss and skipped away singing a happy song.

Sydney pushed past Stanley and stomped off towards the bus stop.

‘I’ve never been so embarrassed in my life. Never ask me to be a sub for you again, Stanley. And don’t bother asking for help with maths either. You won’t get any.’

Stanley stared at the picture on the phone as Sonia found Holly, Caitlin and Rebecca coming through the gates. They formed a group and had a whispered conversation. A few seconds later Stanley heard a chorus of, ‘ooh and aah, and, isn’t that sweet.’

Stanley pointed at the phone and waved it in the air again. His voice became weaker as the girls walked back into school for their extra class.

‘But, I’ve got proof… proof…’

Blooming flowers

Stanley stuck his hands in his pockets and walked slowly round to the florist. The shop was in a precinct about five hundred yards away from the school. A handful of school children were hanging around outside the paper shop eating sweets and drinking pop. Stanley sat on a bench and waited until they moved on. He was already the laughing stock of the school and he would rather wash his face in a bowl full of poisonous frogs than add to his humiliation by being caught in the street with a bunch of flowers.

A tiny bell rang as Stanley opened the door to the florist. He looked around for an assistant amongst the pot plants and vases of cut flowers but saw no one. By the counter was a table with half a dozen bouquets of flowers on it. Stanley read the labels to see if Gran's flowers were among them.

'Yes,' said a shrill, almost squeaky voice.

Stanley looked up to see a thin woman with narrow spectacles perched on a ridiculously long nose, staring down at him. She was wearing a long dress with a flowery print, which was why Stanley had mistaken her for a flower display.

Stanley looked around to make sure he couldn't be overheard.

'I've, er, come to pick up Gran's birthday flowers,' he whispered.

'I didn't hear a word of that,' said the woman.

Stanley checked over his shoulder again in case George or Tall Tim had followed him in. He knew Allergy Alan wouldn't have, he was allergic to flowers.

'I've come to pick up Gran's flowers.'

The florist walked briskly to the counter and picked up her order book.

'Name?'

'Stanley,' said Stanley.

The woman scanned the book.

'No, nothing for Stanley.'

Stanley went bright red.

'They aren't for me,' he choked. 'I'm Stanley. The flowers are for my gran.'

'Why didn't you say?' said the woman. She eyed Stanley with distaste.

'I did say but you…'

'Don't argue, boy. Now, who are the flowers for? What is your unfortunate grandmother's name?'

'I just call her Grandma,' said Stanley.

'Her sur…name… said the woman, slowly.

'I…don't…know,' said Stanley, even more slowly. 'I just call her Grandma.'

The woman sighed, then began to talk to herself.

'It's fine, Christina. You can deal with this.' She looked over her spectacles at Stanley.

'You do know where she lives, I suppose.'

'Yes, of course.'

The woman tapped her foot impatiently.

'Well, are you going to share the information or are we going to stand here all day.'

'Oh, sorry,' said Stanley. 'She lives at 16 Ashton Avenue.'

The woman scanned the list again.

'I have nothing for that address.'

'Well, that's where she lives,' said Stanley.

The woman checked the list again and frowned.

'Are you sure it was your grandmother that ordered the flowers?'

'No,' said Stanley with a sigh. 'Mum ordered them.'

The woman clapped her hand to her forehead.

'Your mother ordered them?'

'Yes,' said Stanley. 'Mrs Stickle. 10 Ashton Avenue.'

The florist glared at Stanley, checked the list, stormed into the back of the shop and returned with the biggest bouquet of flowers that Stanley had ever seen. She pushed them into his hands and frogmarched him to the door.

'Out,' she said. 'And please, please, please, tell your mother that if she needs another bouquet I'd prefer it if she came to pick them up herself.' She pushed Stanley into the street and slammed the door.

Stanley looked up and down the street from behind the bouquet. Luckily, there was no one from his school hanging around. Stanley decided to take the long way home. He couldn't risk catching a bus.

On the way home, Stanley had time to think about things. He decided that the only way he was going to get rid of Soppy Sonia was to get her on her own and explain that he didn't need a girlfriend right now. He worked out a little speech in his head that he thought would convince even the most obstinate girlfriend. It included a bit about the football team he played for having a ban on their players having girlfriends during the football season.

Stanley took a detour to avoid the park and found his way to Sonia's house. As he opened the front gate, he heard a familiar voice.

'Hello, Stanley. Just nipping round with some flowers for the girlfriend are we?'

Stanley's heart sank to the heels of his shoes. He turned round to see Joshua and Harrison grinning at him.

'Flowers, what flowers? Oh… these flowers... Ha, ha, they aren't for Sonia, I mean, Sonia's not my girlfriend; well she thinks she is but she isn't… Anyway, they aren't for her,' he ended lamely.

Joshua opened the gate.

'Off you go then, Stanley. We'll just wait here until you come back. Then we'll know.'

Stanley walked down Sonia's path shaking his head. Things were getting worse by the minute. At the front door, Stanley rang the bell and stood back with the flowers held in front.

A smiling, round faced woman opened the door.

'Hello,' said Stanley politely. 'Is Sonia in? I just needed a word.'

'Are you Stanley?' the woman gushed. 'Sonia told me all about you.'

Stanley groaned. He could imagine what Sonia had said.

'I've, er, just... Is she in?'

'I'm afraid not,' said Sonia's mum. Her eyes lit up as she spotted the flowers. 'Ooh, are those for Sonia? What a lovely thought.' She snatched the flowers from Stanley's hands and stuck her nose into them.

'What a lovely bouquet. Thank you so much. I'll give them to her when she gets home. She'll be thrilled.'

She closed the door leaving Stanley opening and closing his mouth like a goldfish.

Stanley scratched his head and wondered what to do. He couldn't ask for them back now. He needed a plan, and quickly.

When Stanley got back to the gate, Joshua and Harrison were waiting for him.

'I thought you said they weren't for Soppy Sonia, Stanley?' said Harrison.

'They aren't, I was er, just dropping them off. They were for her mother. I've um, got a delivery job at the florist.'

'Of course you have,' said Joshua.

'We'll ask Sonia at school tomorrow,' promised Harrison.

'We might have to mention it to everyone else too,' said Joshua.

Stanley headed for home. Tomorrow could wait. What he needed now was a plan to explain where Gran's flowers had disappeared to.

Things go from bad to worse

Stanley racked his brains but couldn't think of a single reasonable excuse he could use to explain what had happened to Gran's flowers. His top three excuses seemed very feeble somehow.

1. A tornado whipped up out of nowhere and blew the blooms away.

2. The flowers gave me hay fever and I sneezed all the heads off.

3. I was mugged by a member of the flower protection society.

When Stanley arrived at his gate, he was still unsure which of the excuses to use. Then he had an idea.

Mrs Bloomer at number 24 had a garden full of flowers. *She wouldn't miss a few, surely.*

Stanley ran to Mrs Bloomer's house and looked over the fence. The whole of the front garden was covered in a blanket of flowers. He didn't have a clue what sort they were, but they looked impressive.

Stanley let himself in through the gate and crawled into a bed of shrubs. He reached up and snapped off a flower at random, then another and another. When he had half a dozen, he crawled through to the next bed and repeated the exercise. Ten minutes late he crawled back to the gate on his knees with both arms full of brightly coloured blooms. As he neared the gate, he bumped into something bony.

'Stanley Stickle, what are you doing in my flower beds?'

Stanley groaned and stood up.

'I was, er, just checking for stuff.'

'Stuff? What kind of stuff?' Mrs Bloomer folded her arms and glared at Stanley.

Stanley's mind raced like a jet engine on turbo boost.

'I was, er, I was looking for bugs.'

'Bugs? What kind of bugs?'

Stanley shuffled his feet and looked at Mrs Bloomer with what he hoped was a serious face.

'There have been sightings of the Giant Mongolian Sabre-toothed Greenfly,' he said.

'The Giant Mongolian Sabre-toothed Greenfly? I've never heard of it,' said Mrs Bloomer.

'Not many people have. It's new,' said Stanley. 'But some people are infested with them and they don't know. They can eat through a whole bed of flowers in seconds.'

Mrs Bloomer began to look worried.

'Have you found any?'

'No, but they might have laid some eggs on your plants. The professor asked me to get as many blooms as I could and take them to his lab.'

'Professor? Lab? Where is this lab?' Mrs Bloomer looked very concerned.

Stanley tried his hardest to think of a name.

'Professor Plum,' he said.

'Professor Plum? Isn't he a character in the game of Cluedo?'

Stanley thought about it for a moment.

'Yes, I think he does that too. Anyway, got to go, better get these samples back before the eggs hatch and the bugs eat them all.'

Mrs Bloomer stepped away from the gate and hurried down her path in case any of the bugs landed on her.

'What do they look like, Stanley. I'll keep my eye out for them.'

'They're huge,' said Stanley. 'You can't miss them. They're about six inches long and they have long horns and two sets of really pointy teeth that could bite through a steel bar. Oh, and they have red and yellow striped bodies and a bright green head.'

Mrs Bloomer shuddered.

'I'll get my bug sprayer out.'

'I wouldn't bother if I were you,' said Stanley. 'They're immune to all the bug sprays. That's why Professor Damson needs to get fresh samples every day.'

'I thought his name was Professor Plum,' said Mrs Bloomer, suspiciously.

'It is,' said Stanley hurriedly. 'He lives in Damson House. I got a bit confused just then.' Stanley backed off through the gate. 'Right, goodnight, Mrs Bloomer, I wouldn't tell anyone about this if I were you. We don't want to start a panic.'

Stanley turned and ran for home. He sat in the greenhouse, arranged the flowers the best he could and wrapped them in a sheet of newspaper he pulled out of the recycle bin. Stanley took a deep breath, opened the back door and stepped into the kitchen.

Stanley dumped the flowers on the table and ran for the stairs. He hadn't reached half way when he heard his mother's voice.

'Stanley, get back here, please.'

Stanley stopped dead then walked backwards down the six steps. Mum was waiting for him at the bottom of the stairs. She was holding the flowers.

'That florist shop has gone downhill, hasn't it?' Flowers wrapped in newspaper.'

'It's all she had,' said Stanley. 'We were lucky to get that. Good job the florist is next door to a newsagent.'

'And isn't it a coincidence that someone has done the crossword and filled in exactly the same clues that I filled in… and look, they even worked out the anagram clue in the margin, just like I did…*YESTERDAY*.'

Stanley looked at his feet and said nothing.

'And, isn't it an amazing coincidence that the flowers they sent me are EXACTLY the same varieties that Mrs Bloomer grows in her garden?'

Stanley's head came up slowly.

'I can explain, Mum.'

Mrs Stickle took Stanley by the ear and led him into the kitchen. She laid the flowers on the table and sat him down in front of them.

'This had better be *spectacularly* good, Stanley Stickle.'

Twenty minutes later Stanley found himself at Soppy Sonia's gate again. He was carrying the flowers he picked from Mrs Bloomer's garden and the angry words of Mrs

Stickle were still ringing in his ears. Thankfully, she had phoned Soppy Sonia's mum to explain.

Stanley was about to open the gate when he heard giggling behind him.

'Oh, Stanley you are sweet,' said Caitlin. 'Sonia's had two bunches of flowers in one day.'

'Three bunches,' said Rebecca. 'Sydney gave her some daisies too.'

Caitlin positioned herself between Stanley and the gate.

'Nice flowers, Stanley, you must really love Sonia.'

Rebecca giggled and began to sing.

'Stanley loves Sonia, Stanley loves Sonia.'

Stanley pushed past Caitlin and ran down to Sonia's front door. It opened as soon as he put his finger on the bell. Sonia and her mother marched out onto the doorstep. Sonia handed Gran's flowers back and took the new offering.

'They're not as nice as the other ones,' moaned Sonia's mum.

Sonia studied them, then took a sniff.

'These look just like the ones in Mrs Bloomer's garden, Stanley.'

Stanley coughed. 'Do they? I suppose flowers are flowers, they grow everywhere, really.'

'Mrs Bloomer has Giant Mongolian Sabre-toothed Greenfly in her garden, so I hope these didn't come from there.' Sonia's mum examined the flowers suspiciously.

Stanley's chin hit the floor. 'How do you know about the Giant Mongolian Sabre-toothed Greenfly?'

'Everyone's talking about them,' said Sonia. 'You ought to be really careful, Stanley, you live near her. They have six-inch teeth and eat iron bars for breakfast.'

Stanley backed away slowly.

'I'll be careful. I don't think they eat iron bars though.'

'Oh they do, Stanley. Mrs Bottlebrush told us. She said that Mr Snapper the photographer warned her about them down at the allotments. He said he'd heard about them from Mr Fork who lives next door to Mrs Bloomer. The whole town is talking about it.'

Stanley screwed his face up and turned to leave. Things were going downhill faster than a snowball down a ski slope.

'Thanks for the flowers, Stanley,' cooed Sonia. 'Oh, hang on a moment.'

Stanley looked on in horror as Soppy Sonia skipped forward and took hold of his arm. She held the flowers in front of her like a wedding bouquet while her mum took a series of photographs.

'It's a digital camera, Stanley,' said Sonia happily. 'I'll email some copies to you when Dad downloads them to the computer later on. I'll be busy tonight. I have *so* many emails to send.'

Stanley walked home dejectedly. He had to put an end to this. He didn't need just any old plan now. He needed a mega plan, a master plan; a foolproof plan. A plan so cunning you could stick a red brush on it and call it a fox. He was desperate now. So desperate that he had to consider the unthinkable. He was going to have to ask his sister to help.

Stanley gets some advice

Stanley's dinner was in the microwave when he got home. Everyone else had eaten. Stanley warmed it up, ate half of it and scraped the rest into the food-waste bin. He washed his plate in the sink and pushed it into the rack on the draining board to dry. While he was pouring himself a glass of milk, Stacey came into the kitchen.

'Would you like a glass of milk, Sis?' he asked.

Stacey looked at him suspiciously.

'No, not if you're pouring it, I don't know what else you'll put in it.'

Stanley looked shocked.

'Here, have mine,' he offered.

Stacey sniffed it then handed it back.

'You take a sip first. I don't trust you, Stanley.'

Stanley took a big mouthful, gargled with it and then swallowed it with a gulp.

'See, nothing wrong.'

Stacey took the milk back and had a sip.

'What are you after, Stanley? You're never nice to me unless you want something.'

Stanley's eyes opened wide.

'Nothing, nothing at all, Stace.'

'You never call me Stace, I'm getting very nervous now.'

Stanley laughed in an offhand sort of way. 'Would you like a biscuit with the milk?'

Stacey backed off. 'Mum, Stanley's scaring me, he's gone all strange.'

Stanley closed the kitchen door and turned around slowly. 'Well, actually, now you mention it, there is one little thing.'

Stacey pulled out a chair and sat down at the table.

'Okay, out with it. But believe me, Stanley, I'm not lending you any money and I'm not going to do your homework for you.'

'It's nothing like that, Sis. I just need a bit of advice.'

Stacey's bottom jaw hit the table. 'You're asking me for advice?'

'It's girl stuff, Stacey. I'm lumbered with Soppy Sonia and I don't know how to get rid of her. I'm the butt of all the jokes at school, I've tried to get rid of her but I've run out of ideas.'

Stacey shook her head.

'I've heard all about it, Stanley. I would normally tell you to sort it out yourself but it's becoming embarrassing for me too. Even people in my class are laughing at you.'

This time Stanley's jaw hit the table. 'People in your class?' Stacey was two years older than Stanley and at a different school.

'As I see it you have two ways out. You can make sure she goes off you by doing things that girls hate, or, you can stay away from her for two weeks.'

'Two weeks? Why two weeks?'

'It's the rules,' said Stacey. 'As long as you aren't away on holiday, or off sick or something and you don't walk your girlfriend or boyfriend home, or spend time with them for two weeks, then it proves you're no longer together.'

Stanley's face lit up. 'Does it? Just two weeks. Are you sure? I mean, it's not three weeks or a month, or fifteen days or something? I have to get this exactly right.'

'It's two weeks, Stanley. Ask anyone.'

Stanley rushed round to Stacey's side of the table and gave her a huge hug. Stacey screamed and leapt to her feet. 'Get off me, you weirdo.'

Stanley's mum came into the kitchen to see what the fuss was about, so Stanley hugged her too. Mum took advantage of the situation to give Stanley a kiss on the cheek.

Stanley pulled a face and wiped his wet cheek. *Why do mums have to kiss their kids all the time?*

'See you tomorrow, Mum, I'm going up to do my homework and get an early night.'

Mrs Stickle felt Stanley's forehead. 'Oh, dear, Stanley, are you ill again already?'

'No, Mum, I'm on top of the world.' Stanley gave a manic laugh and took the stairs two at a time.

A shiny new plan

When he got to his room, Stanley closed the door, drew the curtains, switched his bedside light on, although it was still light outside, and pulled his notebook out of the drawer. Stanley licked the end of his pencil and went into *think* mode. Twenty minutes later he had a list of all the things he could think of that girls might hate.

1. Football
2. Xbox Last Man Standing, wrestling game
3. Spiders
4. Worms, snakes, frogs, slugs or anything squidgy
5. Mud and dirt
6. Two-headed aliens that have puss oozing from their skin, green eyes, tentacles and a slot for a mouth
7. Cat poo
8. Bugs. All of them
9. Bogies

10. Watching boys eat. (Stacey always goes on about this)

Stanley checked through his list carefully trying to find the two or three things most likely to work. He was sad to cross the two-headed alien off the list but he felt he had to as he didn't know where he could get hold of one. He reluctantly scratched cat poo, but only because he didn't want to carry it around in his pocket all day at school.

In the end, he was left with:

1. Spiders, (big hairy ones)
2. Worms, frogs, slugs
3. Bugs. All kinds

Stanley thought he had a good chance of getting rid of Sonia if she knew that he had a spider to hand or a slug or two in his lunchbox. He decided to catch Boris, a huge spider that he had shared his bedroom with all summer. Boris had fixed an enormous web between the top of his wardrobe and the ceiling. Stanley had to stand on a chair to catch him. Boris was so heavy that when he ran across the top of the wardrobe it sounded like he had boots on.

Stanley sat on the bed and let Boris run up his arm once or twice. The spider did make a bid for freedom but Stanley caught it as it tried to run under his pillow.

Stanley emptied out the matchbox where he kept his old nail clippings, slipped Boris in and closed it. (Stanley kept his nail clippings where he could find them because he had once read a horror story about a boy who was turned into a zombie by a witch doctor who stole nail clippings from the boy's bedroom floor.)

Stanley went to the bathroom, picked up the soap tray from the sink and dried it on the flannel. Then he tipped his clippings into it and put it in his bedside drawer.

He checked that Boris was still safely ensconced in the matchbox and slipped it into his coat pocket ready for school the next day.

All he needed now was a couple of slugs and some beetles.

The beetles were easy. Stanley's mum had a bit of what she called her *wilderness area* at the bottom of their garden. It was a place where she grew nettles and other weeds to attract butterflies and creatures that liked to get stung. In the middle of the nettles was an old log under which there were hundreds of beetles, ants and woodlice. It only took Stanley a few seconds to collect a handful. He dropped them into a small padded bag, switched on his torch and headed for the boggy bit of the garden where the slugs lived.

Stanley soon found two perfect specimens. They were about four inches long and so slimy that they slipped out of his hands when he tried to pick them up. In the end, he had to catch them in his hanky.

Stanley on the news

Stanley got the shock of his life when he walked out of his front gate the next morning. The whole street was filled with TV cameras and reporters. Sky TV had a big van with a satellite dish on top parked outside Gran's house, just down the road. Two burly policemen stood sentry outside his house. As soon as Stanley stepped foot onto the street there was a mad rush to get to him first.

'Stanley, over here.'

'No, here, Stanley, talk to the BBC.'

'Sky were here first, Stanley, talk to us.'

Stanley looked around with his mouth hanging open. The only time he'd seen anything like this was on TV when they were covering an opening night of a new film.

Eventually the policemen got some control. The newspapermen crowded in as close as they could get as Stanley was ushered in front of the Sky TV camera by a broad-shouldered man with thick, curly eyebrows.

'Stand here, Stanley. Don't move, there's a good lad. I'll just do an intro and we'll get on with the interview, okay?'

Stanley nodded. He looked around at all the flashing cameras and began to feel more than a little bit nervous. *What did they want? Surely they didn't know about Soppy Sonia. If the story was on the news he was going to run away to sea.*

The presenter smoothed down his curly eyebrows and positioned himself in front of the camera.

'Hello, I'm Steve Slurry and I'm here in the sleepy little town of Deadenbury in the East Midlands. The newspaper headlines in this place are usually made up of, "cat stuck in tree," or, "crop circle found on traffic roundabout," but today the town has woken up to the news that the deadly, Giant Mongolian Sabre-toothed Greenfly has invaded their gardens. With me, is the young boy who helped the secretive and mysterious, Professor Plum, capture these monstrous insects. Tell me, Stanley, when did you first see one of these creatures?'

As the camera pointed towards Stanley, he became suddenly aware of a pain in his tummy; a pain that made him want to run for the toilet. His stomach began to bubble, then it began to rumble. The presenter pushed his microphone under his nose. Stanley held his tummy and made an *eeeugh*, sort of noise. His knees turned to jelly; he hiccupped and put his hand to his mouth.

'Come on, Stanley, don't be shy,' said the reporter. 'There are millions of viewers waiting to hear what you discovered. Out with it.'

Unfortunately for the cameraman, the only thing that came out of Stanley was a huge projectile of vomit. It hit the camera squarely on the lens and splattered all over the road.

The reporters stepped back but continued to scribble on their notepads. Stanley's face went a funny green colour as he turned towards the presenter.

'No, no, careful, son, don't…'

Stanley vomited again, all over the presenter's shirt.

Stanley looked around helplessly but no one came to his assistance. Then a policeman stepped forward. He knelt down next to Stanley took off his helmet, and placed it on the floor next to him.

'Are you alright now, Stanley? Feeling better, Son?'

Stanley nodded, smiled, then threw up in the policeman's helmet.

The crowd backed off again. Stanley wiped his mouth. The reporters kept their distance; one or two began to feel ill themselves.

'STANLEEEEEEEEE!' A cross between a screech and a scream filled the air.

Stanley cringed. He knew that voice. Only one person could hit that particular note. He turned to see his gran standing on the rim of the circle of reporters. Stanley edged towards her, careful not to take his eyes off the cameramen.

'Stanley,' said Gran. 'What are you doing on Sky TV? Get off it this instant.'

'I'd like to, Gran,' said Stanley, seriously. 'But they want to talk to me about something.'

Gran looked sternly at Stanley. 'What have been up to, young man?'

'Nothing, Gran,' Stanley tried to look innocent.

Gran decided to believe him. She turned to face the reporters.

'Leave him alone, you lot. It wasn't him, whatever he's supposed to have done. Haven't you got better things to do?'

'He's the big story of the day,' said the woman from the Daily Mirror.

'He's top billing,' said the reporter from The Times.

'Come on, Stanley, the world is waiting,' said the woman from Knitters Weekly.

Gran gave Stanley a sloppy wet kiss on the cheek. Stanley wiped off the slobber with his sleeve as he walked back to face the press. *Why do grandmas want to kiss you all the time?*

Stanley's mum arrived on the scene with a bowl of water, a couple of flannels and a handful of towels. The Sky team cleaned up their camera while the presenter went into Stanley's house to clean himself up. When he had wiped the sick from his suit jacket he persuaded Stanley's mum to lend him one of Mr Stickle's shirts and, fifteen minutes after the vomiting began, he was back out on the street pointing the microphone at Stanley.

‘Right, Stanley. You aren’t going to be sick again, are you?’

Stanley shook his head.

The presenter went through his intro again and asked Stanley a question.

‘Stanley, who is this mysterious professor?’

Stanley squirmed and tried to think fast.

‘I, er, don’t know him that well, I only saw him once or twice.’

‘A real mystery man, hey? When did you first meet him?’

‘It was, er, the other day, he had a net and was catching stuff and I asked what he was catching, so he told me.’

‘I see, and did he have a Giant Mongolian Sabre-toothed Greenfly in his net?’

‘Yes… I mean, he must have, I suppose. There was something wriggling about in there.’

‘And he told you what he’d caught?’

‘Yes, he said it was a Giant Mongolian Sabre-toothed Greenfly and they were highly dangerous. He said they shouldn’t be approached unless you wore those gloves like knights in armour wear.’

‘And was he wearing metal knight’s gloves, Stanley?’

Stanley began to get carried away.

‘Yes, and he had a helmet too and a hor… no he didn’t have a horse, but he had a long sharp lance to poke the giant greenfly with. It makes them jump so he can catch them in his net.’

The press gang rushed forward. They all began to ask questions at once.

‘What did they look like?’

‘How big were their teeth?’

‘Can they really bite through concrete?’

‘Can I use your toilet; I need a wee?’

The policemen stepped in to calm the situation down and Stanley was again pushed in front of the camera. The Sky man waited for silence then stuck the microphone in Stanley’s face again.

'One last question, Stanley, then we'll let you go to school. I'm sure you'll be very popular today.'

Stanley screwed his face up. He hadn't thought of that. *Everyone will have seen him on TV.*

'Where is the professor now, Stanley? We really need to talk to him.'

'Oh, he's off exploring again I expect. He'll be Austria, or France, probably, somewhere with a jungle.' Geography wasn't Stanley's best subject.

The Sky team turned away from Stanley and began to run up the road toward Mrs Bloomer's house. The rest of the reporters followed, chattering into digital recorders and jotting down notes. Mrs Bloomer was waiting for them at her gate. She was wearing her best frock and pearls.

Stanley took the opportunity to sneak off. He walked briskly past the sound crew who were wiping the last bits of vomited carrot from their cables and slipped through the entry that led out onto the avenue at the back of his house.

Stanley walked to school with his mind in turmoil. He didn't know which of the two messes he was in was worse and which one he'd rather be out of first. *Sonia probably*, the thought of kissing her was far worse than throwing up on a TV crew. He would rather be covered in honey and eaten alive by a colony of soldier ants than kiss Sonia again.

When Stanley reached the school gates, he found the entire school population waiting for him. As he walked into the playground, someone began to clap, by the time he'd gone five yards he was being applauded and cheered as though he'd just won a gold medal in the 800 metres at the Olympics.

Stanley Stickle does NOT have a girlfriend

At morning assembly, Stanley was called out to the front where the headmaster made a little speech praising his attributes. He stood there while they sang the school song and while the deputy head gave a long, boring speech about public spirit and endeavour.

Stanley was still the main topic of conversation at lunchtime. Everywhere he went he was followed by a crowd of admirers.

'Tell us again how you threw up on the camera, Stanley.'

'Stanley, have you got any Giant Mongolian Sabre-toothed Greenfly eggs at home?'

Stanley headed for the corridor outside the head's office to escape the constant attention. No pupil ever hung around outside the head's office unless they had been sent for.

Stanley sat down next to a coffee table with school promotional leaflets all over it and tried to think. He had to find a way to get Sonia on her own at some point that afternoon. He patted his pocket to make sure he still had Boris's matchbox and idly pushed the leaflets about. He thought about telling Sonia that he had a Giant Mongolian Sabre-toothed Greenfly in his pocket instead of Boris, but she might just ask to see it.

He was brought out of his contemplation by Mrs Oscar, the drama teacher.

'Well, if it isn't the hero of the hour. Hello, Stanley. Are you sure I can't persuade you to be in the school production this year? It would be lovely to have a star name in the lead role.'

Stanley choked. He would rather sit on a cushion made of cactus than star in the school drama production. He shook his head, pointed to his throat and croaked.

'Sorry, I've got this tonsil thing and it never goes away. I couldn't possibly sing.'

Mrs Oscar's smile faded.

'That's a shame, Stanley. Mrs Crochet told me you had a beautiful singing voice. She had you in the junior choir a couple of years ago, didn't she?'

'I was younger then,' croaked Stanley. 'All that singing wore my tonsils out.'

Mrs Oscar patted Stanley on the head.

'Ah well, if you change your mind you know where we are.' She handed Stanley a leaflet. 'This will tell you all about it. We practice every night after school and on Saturday mornings. You would be made very welcome, we're *desperate* for boys. I really can't understand why they don't want to take part.'

Stanley knew exactly why boys didn't want to take part. He would rather crawl over a bed of hot coals than be laughed at by every child in the school.

Stanley stuffed the leaflet into his pocket and made his way back to class.

When he arrived, he was roundly booed by his classmates. The teacher grabbed hold of his collar and marched him back to where he had just come from; the head's office.

'Stanley Stickle, you have brought shame and disgrace upon this school.'

The head wasn't happy. Stanley could tell. He decided to ask what he had done wrong. He was a hero a few short hours ago.

'You are all over the TV again, Stanley. But for a different reason this time. It appears that the journalists have done some investigating at the National History Museum. It turns out that there is no such thing as a Giant

Mongolian Sabre-toothed Greenfly. What do you have to say to that?'

'Professor Plum told me that there was, and…'

The headmaster slammed his hand down on the desk so hard that his desk diary shot up into the air.

'There is no Professor Plum, Stanley Stickle. There never was a Professor Plum. You made it all up, didn't you? Come on, admit it.'

Stanley hung his head and looked at his shoes.

'I only did it because…' (Stanley thought it best not to mention stealing Mrs Bloomer's flowers,) because… I… I don't know why I said all that really. I didn't expect the TV cameras to show up and I didn't expect to be treated like a celeb…'

'Enough.' The headmaster slammed his hand down again. 'Stanley Stickle, you will apologise to the whole school at assembly tomorrow morning and this ridiculous incident will go down on your school record. Now, get back to your class and try to think of a way by which you can make amends.'

Stanley endured a miserable afternoon of name-calling. It was even worse than the insults he got when his fellow pupils found out about Sonia. The only bright spot was that Soppy Sonia might want to give him up now he wasn't famous anymore.

His hopes were dashed when he walked out of school and found her waiting for him. She held out her bag for him to carry. Stanley ignored her outstretched arm and walked past.

Sonia caught up with Stanley at the war memorial by the shopping precinct. He sat on the steps and Sonia sat beside him.

'Oh, Stanley, I do feel sorry for you.'

Stanley flinched as she laid her hand on his arm. He pushed his hand into his pocket. Now was the time for Boris to get in on the act. He pulled out the matchbox and faced Sonia.

'You haven't met Boris yet, have you?'

Soppy Sonia shook her head. 'No, who is Boris?'

Stanley grinned an evil grin and pushed the box open. Boris woke up immediately and began to crawl out. Sonia screamed.

'Oh, Stanley, isn't he gorgeous. Can I hold him?'

Stanley was shocked. *Sonia couldn't like spiders, surely.*

'Go on, Stanley, I love spiders. I held a tarantula once.'

Stanley closed the matchbox and shoved it back in his pocket. *Okay, she liked spiders but what about slugs?*

Stanley opened his lunch box and held it out for Sonia to see. The two fat slugs were nibbling on a wet piece of lettuce.

Sonia screamed again.

'Oh, Stanley, what lovely slugs, are they for me? I *adore* slugs; they feel lovely and slimy. Can I hold one?'

Stanley was staggered. *A girl who likes spiders and slugs? This was impossible.*

Stanley reached into his pocket to get the padded bagful of bugs.

'I suppose you like wood lice and beetles too?'

'Not really,' said Sonia. 'I don't mind them, but they aren't as much fun as spiders and slugs.'

Stanley gave up. Sonia had beaten him. There was no way he was going to get rid of her now.

As he pushed the bag of insects back into his pocket, his hand came into contact with something smooth. He pulled out the school concert leaflet and walked to the litter bin to throw it away. Then he had a brainwave. His eyes scanned the leaflet. The concert didn't take place for three months and there was practice *every night* after school until then. *Three long, lovely months, and he only needed two weeks*. Stanley turned around sharply and stepped quickly back to Soppy Sonia.

'Sonia, I meant to tell you that I won't be able to see you anymore.'

'Don't be silly, Stanley, of course you will. I'm never off school.'

'I can't, Sonia, honestly. I've been asked to play the lead role in the school production and that means after-school practice every night for three months. They practice on Saturdays too, so I won't be able to see you then either.' Stanley crossed his fingers tightly and hoped.

Sonia looked sad. Then her face lit up. 'I'll join too; we can be in it together.'

Stanley shook his head. 'I'm afraid they don't want any more girls, Sonia. It's only boys they need. Mrs Oscar is desperate to sign me up.'

'Oh bother,' said Sonia. 'That means we won't be going out together anymore, because if we don't see each other for two weeks, it's all off.'

Stanley tried to act surprised.

'Does it? That's a shame. Ah well, I suppose all good things come to an end.'

Sonia leaned forward to kiss him on the cheek. Stanley fell backwards and rolled out of the way. *What was it with girls? Why did they have to keep kissing people?*

Sonia got to her feet. 'I don't know what I'm going to do now, I'm sure. I suppose I'd better start looking for a new boyfriend.'

Stanley nodded in agreement. He couldn't stop nodding. He looked like one of those nodding dogs that some people have on the parcel shelf of their cars.

'Hey, I know just the person for you,' he said eventually. 'What about Sydney? He likes you. He wanted to be my substitute.'

Sonia thought for a second. 'Yes, he did, didn't he? And he gave me flowers. That was sweet of him.' She looked around at the crowd of children milling about. She spotted him sitting at the bus stop studying his math's book.

'Sydney,' she called. 'I've changed my mind; will you walk me home?'

Stanley whooped and punched the air. He had finally got rid of Soppy Sonia. He had to be careful though. He couldn't take any chances. *She might want him back if he broke the rules.*

Stanley read the leaflet again and walked back into school. He found Mrs Oscar fussing around a group of kids in the hall. He let the door slam behind him to announce his entrance.

'Mrs Oscar,' he said. 'My tonsils appear to have got better this afternoon. I'd like to join the production.'

Mrs Oscar was delighted. She sat Stanley down on the corner of the stage and ran off to find him a script.

Stanley was really pleased with himself. *Things are looking up.* He could put up with this for a while but he had no intention of walking onto the stage on opening night. Stanley would rather swim across a river full of starving piranhas than be the star turn when the curtain went up. What he needed was a plan to get him out of the production in two weeks' time.

Stanley grinned as the germ of a plan sneaked into his brain. It needed work, but it was a start. He smiled his best smile as he took the script from Mrs Oscar, then he pulled out his pen and scribbled, Master Plan, on the inside page. Mrs Oscar sat at the piano and began to play the opening bars of the *Consider Yourself*, song. Stanley tore two thin strips of paper from the edge of the script, screwed them into tiny balls and stuck them in his ears to drown out the racket. Then he scratched his head, sucked on the end of his pen and began to think.

THE END